A Note from Michelle about

CAMP HIDE-A-PET

Hi! I'm Michelle Tanner. I'm nine years old, and I'm going to Camp Wildwood for a whole week! There's just one problem. I have nobody to watch my guinea pig, Sunny, while I'm away.

Bringing pets to Camp Wildwood is against the rules. But I can't leave my guinea pig all alone! That's why I have to find a really good hiding place for Sunny as soon as I get there. Or else I'm toast!

I wish I could ask my family for help. I bet they'd have lots of great ideas. That's because I have lots of people in my family!

There's my dad and my two older sisters, D.J. and Stephanie. But that's not all.

My mom died when I was little. So my uncle Jesse moved in to help Dad take care of us. So did Joey Gladstone. He's my dad's friend from college. It's almost like having three dads. But that's still not all!

First Uncle Jesse got married to Becky Donaldson. Then they had twin boys, Nicky and Alex. The twins are four years old now. And they're so cute.

That's nine people. And our dog, Comet, makes ten. Sure, it gets kind of crazy sometimes. But I wouldn't change it for anything. It's so much fun living in a full house!

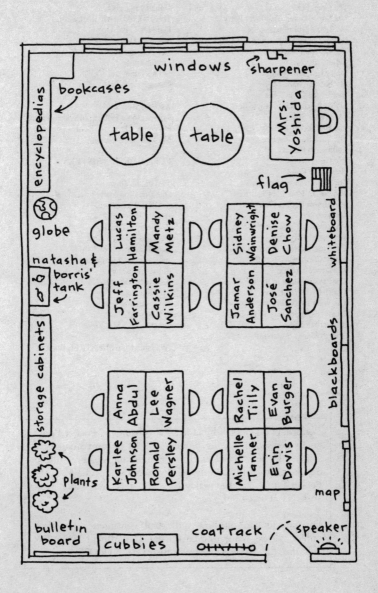

windows
sharpener
encyclopedias
bookcases
table
table
Mrs. Yoshida
flag
globe
natasha & borris' tank
whiteboard
Lucas Hamilton
Mandy Metz
Sidney Wainwright
Denise Chow
Jeff Farrington
Cassie Wilkins
Jamar Anderson
José Sanchez
storage cabinets
blackboards
Anna Abdul
Lee Wagner
Rachel Tilly
Evan Burger
Karlee Johnson
Ronald Persley
Michelle Tanner
Erin Davis
plants
map
bulletin board
cubbies
coat rack
speaker

FULL HOUSE™ MICHELLE novels

The Great Pet Project
The Super-Duper Sleepover Party
My Two Best Friends
Lucky, Lucky Day
The Ghost in My Closet
Ballet Surprise
Major League Trouble
My Fourth-Grade Mess
Bunk 3, Teddy and Me
My Best Friend Is a Movie Star!
    (Super Special)
The Big Turkey Escape
The Substitute Teacher
Calling All Planets
I've Got a Secret
How to Be Cool
The Not-So-Great Outdoors
My Ho-Ho-Horrible Christmas
My Almost Perfect Plan
April Fools!
My Life Is a Three-Ring Circus
Welcome to My Zoo
The Problem with Pen Pals
Merry Christmas, World!
Tap Dance Trouble
The Fastest Turtle in the West
The Baby-sitting Boss
The Wish I Wish I Never Wished
Pigs, Pies, and Plenty of Problems
If I Were President
How to Meet a Superstar

Unlucky in Lunch
There's Gold in My Backyard!
Field Day Foul-Up
Smile and Say "Woof!"
The Penguin Skates
For the Birds
Is This Funny, or What?
Camp Hide-a-Pet

Activity Books

My Awesome Holiday Friendship Book
My Super Sleepover Book
My Year of Fun Book

FULL HOUSE™ SISTERS

Two on the Town
One Boss Too Many
And the Winner Is . . .
How to Hide a Horse
Problems in Paradise
Will You Be My Valentine?
Let's Put On a Show!
Baby-sitters & Company
Substitute Sister
Ask Miss Know-It-All
Matchmakers
No Rules Weekend
A Dog's Life
Once Upon a Mix-Up

Available from MINSTREL Books

For orders other than by individual consumers, Pocket Books grants a discount on the purchase of **10 or more** copies of single titles for special markets or premium use. For further details, please write to the Vice President of Special Markets, Pocket Books, 1230 Avenue of the Americas, 9th Floor, New York, NY 10020-1586.

For information on how individual consumers can place orders, please write to Mail Order Department, Simon & Schuster, Inc., 100 Front Street, Riverside, NJ 08075.

FULL HOUSE™

Michelle
and Friends

CAMP HIDE-A-PET

Cathy East Dubowski

A Parachute Press Book

A
MINSTREL®
BOOK

Published by POCKET BOOKS
New York   London   Toronto   Sydney   Singapore

A MINSTREL PAPERBACK *Original*

A Minstrel Book published by
POCKET BOOKS, a division of Simon & Schuster, Inc.
1230 Avenue of the Americas, New York, NY 10020

A PARACHUTE PRESS BOOK

™ Copyright © and ™ 2001 by Warner Bros.

FULL HOUSE, characters, names and all related indicia are
trademarks of Warner Bros. © 2001.

ISBN: 0-671-04204-1

First Minstrel Books printing July 2001

10   9   8   7   6   5   4   3   2   1

A MINSTREL BOOK and colophon are registered trademarks of
Simon & Schuster, Inc.

Printed in the U.S.A.

CAMP HIDE-A-PET

Chapter

1

♥ "There's the bus, Dad!" nine-year-old Michelle Tanner shouted as she stared out the window of her family's car. "Hurry!"

"Don't worry, Michelle," Danny Tanner replied with a chuckle. "I'm sure they won't leave without you."

School was out and Michelle was on her way to summer camp for a whole week!

Her father had brought her to the Fraser Elementary School parking lot to meet the Camp Wildwood bus. The place was mobbed with kids and parents saying goodbye.

Soon Michelle would be on that bus heading out of the city and into the country, where the sky was clear and the world was green. Michelle couldn't wait! She hoped she would make some cool new friends.

Danny parked the van and got Michelle's trunk out of the back. "Now, don't forget," he told Michelle. "Each day's outfit is already packed in a resealable plastic bag. So on Monday, all you have to do is pull out the bag marked Monday. Then on Tuesday, you pull out—"

"I get it, Dad," Michelle said. She rolled her eyes, but had to laugh. Her dad was really into being neat and organized. Sometimes he was a little *too* into it.

Danny carried Michelle's trunk over to the side of the bus so it could be loaded. Most of the other girls had trunks, too, just like Michelle's older sister Stephanie said they would. Stephanie had given Michelle her old camp trunk. Stuff didn't get squashed in them, like with duffel bags. They made great tables beside the bunks, too.

Danny chatted with one of the counselors for a few minutes. Then he turned back to Michelle. "Goodbye, pumpkin," he told her. "Have fun. Call me on my cell phone if you need anything. Okay?"

"Don't worry, Dad," Michelle said. "I'll be fine."

Michelle hugged her father goodbye and watched him drive away. Then she grabbed her backpack and started to climb onto the bus.

"Michelle! Wait!" someone called.

Michelle whirled around. Her friend Lee Wagner had just hopped out of his parents' car. His glasses slipped down his nose as he ran to catch up with her.

Lee was going to pet-sit Michelle's black-and-white guinea pig, Sunny, while Michelle was at camp.

How nice, Michelle thought. Lee brought Sunny to say goodbye to me. He's the best friend ever.

Lee stopped short in front of her. He sucked in a deep breath. "Michelle, I can't keep Sunny!" he blurted out.

Michelle stared at him. "What?"

"I'm sorry. I just can't watch Sunny this week," Lee repeated. "My folks say we have to go visit my aunt in Oklahoma. She just had twins. They're early."

"No way!" Michelle cried. "You promised!"

"I know." Lee squirmed. "I can't help it. I have to go with my parents." He shoved Sunny into Michelle's arms. "I promise I'll watch him next time, okay?"

A car horn honked, and Lee glanced over his shoulder. "Sorry, Michelle. I have to go. Bye!"

Michelle stared at Lee as he dashed back to his car. She was speechless.

Michelle glanced down at Sunny. Sunny gazed up at Michelle and twitched his whiskers.

Michelle sighed. Now what am I going to do?

Her best friend Cassie Wilkins couldn't look after Sunny. She was away on vacation. Her other best friend Mandy Metz couldn't do it, either. Her mom had said no.

Even though Michelle lived in a full house, it was going to be pretty empty this week. Her dad, Danny Tanner, was going away on a business trip until Tuesday night. Her sisters, Stephanie and D.J., were busy with summer jobs, and they were staying at friends' houses until their dad came home.

Uncle Jesse and Aunt Becky, who lived on the third floor of the Tanners' house, would have watched Sunny. Their four-year-old twins, Nicky and Alex, loved to play with the guinea pig. But they had already gone out of town to visit Aunt Becky's family for a few days.

Joey Gladstone, who lived in an apartment in the basement, was leaving the next day for a stand-up comedian convention in Las Vegas.

No one will be around to give Sunny the love and attention he needs, Michelle thought. What do I do now?

After a minute an idea came her. Maybe I can call some other kids in my class. Maybe one of them can take care of Sunny.

Phweet!

A counselor blew a whistle. "Hey, everybody. Listen up!"

The kids quieted down.

"Please line up in single file," the counselor called out. "In three minutes this bus is moving out!"

Oh, no! Michelle thought. There was no time to call anybody, even if she could think of somebody to call.

Michelle gulped. She looked into Sunny's sweet little face. The small furry little animal was so cute and helpless.

There was only one thing to do.

"Don't worry, Sunny," Michelle whispered to her pet. "I'll take care of you.

She slipped Sunny into her backpack.

"You and I are going to camp!"

Chapter 2

♥ "Row, row, row your boat, gently down the stream. Merrily, merrily, merrily, merrily, life is just a dream!" Everyone started singing camp songs as soon as the bus pulled out of the parking lot.

Michelle wanted to join in. But first she had to check on Sunny. She opened the zipper on her backpack just a little and peeked inside.

Was it too hot in there? Could Sunny breathe all right? Michelle saw Sunny's pink nose twitch. He looked just fine. Michelle relaxed back into her seat.

Where will I put Sunny when I get to camp? Michelle wondered. She realized she had no idea. She would have to figure that out when she got there.

Michelle glanced at the girl sitting next to her. She had straight, shoulder-length blond hair and bangs. She looked really nice and friendly.

Maybe I can tell her about Sunny, Michelle thought. But then she realized, what if the girl didn't like guinea pigs? Michelle decided to keep Sunny a secret for now. She tucked her backpack against the wall beside her legs. She hoped the girl wouldn't notice Sunny moving around in there.

"Hi, my name is Megan," the blond girl sitting next to her said with a friendly smile. "Is this your first time at camp?"

"No," Michelle told her. "But it's my first time at Camp Wildwood. How about you?"

"Same here," Megan said. "But my cousin went here last year. She said it's really cool."

"Awesome!" Michelle smiled back at Megan. She had a feeling she would like hanging out with her. Maybe the two of them would be assigned to the same cabin or something.

"Hey, kids!" Two counselors at the front of the bus turned to face the campers. Everyone quieted down. "I'm Lauren," the tall girl with dark blond hair told everyone. She pointed to a shorter girl with a long black ponytail. "And this is Rachael. We're going to have a great time at camp, right?"

"Right!" a bunch of kids hollered.

"Great." Lauren held up a clipboard. "But first we've got a few dos and don'ts to go over. So listen up."

Michelle sat up straight in her seat and paid close attention. She didn't want to break any rules while she was at Camp Wildwood.

"First, there are some things that are not allowed at camp," Lauren said. "No radios, no Gameboys, no candy in the cabins—"

"No candy?" a red-haired girl in front of Michelle repeated. "Why not?"

"Candy and other food attracts raccoons into the cabins," Rachael explained.

"Right," Lauren said. "And even though raccoons look cute, they're wild animals. So let's keep our cabins snack-free."

Lauren continued to read from her list. "Here are some more no-nos: Rollerblades, pets from home—"

Michelle gulped. Did Lauren just say p-p-p-pets?

I didn't know the camp had a rule against pets! Michelle thought. What am I going to do now? She peeked in the top of her backpack. She could see Sunny's cute little black eyes staring back at her. She was glad now that she hadn't told Megan about him.

There's only one thing to do, Michelle decided.

I'm going to have to keep Sunny a secret—for the whole week!

Michelle and Megan peered out the bus window as they drove up to camp. "Yay! We're here!" Megan cheered.

"Wow!" Michelle said. "This place is so cool."

Two main buildings sat in the middle of a grassy, tree-filled area. One had a sign on it that said Dining Hall. The sign in front of the other building read Meeting Room.

To the right a path led to the small cabins that sat nestled in the woods. Each had a view of a long sloping hill that led down to a sparkling lake and a dock for swimming. Through the open side of a boathouse Michelle could see several canoes bobbing in the water.

"Do you like to swim?" Michelle asked Megan.

"Sure!" Megan told her. "I can't wait to jump in that lake."

After the bus parked, the campers filed out and lined up to check in. A counselor checked each person's name off a list, and the camp nurse collected everyone's health form. Then all the campers marched over to the big building labeled Meeting Room.

Once everyone was seated inside, a tan woman with short gray hair stood up at the front of the

9

room. "Welcome to Camp Wildwood," the woman said in a booming voice. "I'm the camp director, Ms. Greene. All of you are going to spend a lot of time outdoors, on the water, and having fun this week!"

Ms. Greene made a few announcements, then called out cabin assignments. "Cabin One—Lateesha Jackson, Krysta Strandberg, Michelle Tanner, Megan Anderson . . ."

That's us, Michelle thought. Let's go, Sunny. She carefully carried her backpack to the front of the room. Seven other girls soon joined her. Everyone smiled shyly at one another.

Michelle was glad to see that Megan, the blond girl from the bus, was going to be in her cabin.

"Counselor for Cabin One, is—Lauren MacKenzie," Ms. Greene announced.

Michelle gulped. Lauren was the one who read out all the rules on the bus. She definitely wouldn't like it if she knew about Sunny.

When all the assignments were made, the counselors led their girls to their cabins. Each building was square with windows all around. Three wooden steps led up to the screen door in each one.

"It's cool being in Cabin One," Lateesha joked. "It means we're number one!"

"Yeah!" a few of the other girls cheered.

"Okay, girls," Lauren said. "Bunk assignments. I

don't care which bunk you choose—as long as there's no arguing, okay?"

Everyone agreed. Michelle chose a bottom bunk, and Megan chose the top bunk above her.

"Now we're going to play a game to help us get to know each other," Lauren said. "It's called Two Truths and a Lie."

Krysta twirled a curly lock of brown hair around her finger. "That's a weird name for a game. How do you play?"

"You go around the circle," Lauren explained. "Each girl tells two things that are true about herself. And one thing that's not. The other girls have to guess which one is not true." Lauren glanced around the room. "Why don't you start, Michelle?"

"Me? Okay." Michelle thought hard. What should she tell everyone?

"I live in a house with eight other people," Michelle said. "I like pepperoni pizza. And I have a guinea pig named Sunny."

Michelle bit her lip. Whoops! Maybe I shouldn't have mentioned Sunny, she thought. She glanced over at her backpack sitting on her bunk.

"It can't be the pizza part," a girl named Anita guessed. "Everybody loves pizza."

The girls whispered among themselves.

At last Krysta said, "We think it's a lie that you live with eight people."

Michelle giggled. "Wrong!" She quickly told them all about her very large family.

"So you don't have a guinea pig?" Taylor asked.

"Wrong again," Michelle said. "I do have a guinea pig and his name is Sunny." What she didn't say out loud was: And I hope none of you figures out that he's right here in this room!

"So you hate pizza?" everybody exclaimed.

"No, I never said I hate all kinds of pizza. Just *pepperoni* pizza," Michelle said with a giggle.

Lauren laughed. "I hate pepperoni pizza, too. Good job, Michelle. You stumped everyone. That was very sneaky!"

Yikes! Michelle thought. I don't want Lauren to think I'm sneaky!

Anita took the next turn at Two Truths and One Lie. Soon Michelle began to relax and play along. The game taught her a lot about her cabin mates.

This was Anita's first time at camp, and she liked to write in her diary. Megan wanted to be a vet, and her favorite color was green. Lateesha was an artist and hated broccoli. Krysta took dance lessons and she played baseball. Taylor and Brianna were both only children. And Jessie loved soccer more than anything.

"Now you all have some free time," Lauren announced at the end of the game. "You can visit the Trading Post if you like. They've got neat stuff for sale. Or you can walk around and get to know the place. But remember our main rule: Always stay with a buddy. Okay?"

"Okay!" everyone answered.

"Don't forget to meet at the lake at four for a swim test," Lauren added. "That's about forty-five minutes from now."

Everyone stampeded out of the cabin—except Michelle.

"Come on, Michelle," Lauren called. She turned around and held open the door.

"Uh—I'll be right there," Michelle said with a bright smile. "I just need to . . . put on some sunscreen. I burn really easily."

"Good idea. See you later!" Lauren let the cabin door swing shut behind her.

"Bye!" Michelle looked around. Thank goodness—all alone! Now she could find the perfect spot for Sunny.

She quickly dug into her backpack. "Sunny. Sunny! Are you all right? Speak to me!"

She pulled Sunny out of her pack. The guinea pig seemed to be perfectly fine. "What a good boy you are!" Michelle crooned as she stroked her pet's soft fur.

"What am I going to do with you?" she murmured. She turned around to lay Sunny on her bed.

She needed to come up with some kind of cage. She'd have to find him something to eat, and something to use for a water bowl, and . . .

"Michelle! What's that?"

Michelle froze. Slowly she turned around. Her bunkmate Megan was standing in the doorway.

She was staring right at Sunny!

Chapter
3

♥ "Megan, please don't tell anybody," Michelle begged. "I'll do anything! I'll make your bunk every day. I'll give you my all of my desserts! I'll—"

"Michelle! Stop!" Megan laughed. "You don't have to do any of that. I'm not going to tell anyone about your pet." She bent down to stroke the guinea pig's soft fur. "What's his name?"

"S-Sunny," Michelle stuttered.

"He is so cute," Megan said. "No wonder you brought him with you."

Michelle explained to Megan that Lee was supposed to pet sit—and that he couldn't at the last minute. Since there was no time to find another petsitter, she just *had* to bring Sunny to camp.

15

"I love animals," Megan said. "We have two golden retrievers at home—Morgan and Macdougal."

"Really?" Michelle said. "We have one, too. His name is Comet."

Megan grinned. "No wonder I like you! Don't worry, Michelle. I'll keep your secret. And I would love to help you take care of Sunny."

"Thanks," Michelle said. "Thanks a lot!"

Megan frowned. "We'll have to be really careful, though. My cousin took her rabbit to camp here last year. The counselors found out, and my cousin got sent home."

"Oh, no!" Michelle said. "That would be awful!"

Megan nodded. "Don't worry. We'll just be really careful."

Suddenly the door to the cabin swung open.

Michelle gulped. Lauren was coming inside!

Megan's back was to the door, so Michelle quickly shoved Sunny into Megan's arms. That way, Lauren wouldn't see him right away. "Quick!" Michelle whispered. "Hide Sunny!"

Michelle hurried over to Lauren. She had to distract her! She held her wrist in front of Lauren's nose. "Um, look, Lauren! See my friendship bracelet?"

Lauren took a step backward. "Uh, very nice, Michelle."

16

Michelle dodged again, trying to block Lauren's view of Megan. "My sister made it for me. Look! She used three colors of thread."

"Cool," Lauren said. "Michelle, can I get by? I need to get something out of my trunk."

Michelle stepped aside. Had Megan hidden Sunny in time?

Megan stood facing Lauren. "Hi!" she said cheerfully.

"I realized I didn't have my sunscreen, either." Lauren pulled a purple bottle out of her trunk. "Don't forget, girls. The swim test for everybody is in half an hour."

"We'll be there!" Michelle said brightly.

The screen door slammed shut as Lauren hurried out of the cabin.

Michelle held her breath and waited until she was sure Lauren was gone. At last she let it out in a big whoosh. "Wow! That was close!"

"I thought we were caught for sure," Megan agreed.

"So, where'd you hide Sunny?" Michelle asked.

"Under there." Megan pointed beneath Michelle's bed. "I wrapped him up in a beach towel that I had put on my bunk."

"Cool." Michelle crawled under the bunk to get Sunny. She spotted the brightly colored towel and lifted it up. But Sunny wasn't there!

Michelle's heart missed a beat. Where could Sunny be? Michelle checked carefully under the bunk. She squinted into the shadowy corners. Still she didn't see Sunny anywhere!

Michelle wiggled out from under the bunk.

"What's wrong?" Megan asked.

"I can't believe it!" Michelle wailed. "Sunny's gone!"

Chapter
4

♥ "No way!" Megan exclaimed. "I put him right here under the bunk!"

"Well, he's not there now!" Michelle pointed out.

"Let's look around," Megan suggested. "He has to be here somewhere."

The two girls searched in every corner of the cabin, but they couldn't find Sunny anywhere.

"Did you check behind your trunk?" Michelle asked.

"Yes!" Megan replied. "And under all the beds!"

"Oh, Sunny," Michelle called. "Where are you?"

"Maybe he got out somehow," Megan guessed.

"I hope not! If he gets lost in the woods, he'll be terrified!" Michelle said. She opened the cabin door looked around. "Which way could he have gone?" she asked.

Just then something scooted between her legs and out the door. "Sunny!" Michelle and Megan shouted at once.

"Come on," Michelle told her new friend. "We've got to catch him before somebody sees him!"

Together the two girls chased after the fat little guinea pig. He stopped right in front of a nearby cabin.

"Now we've got you!" Michelle said. Just as she was about to reach down to pick him up, the door to the cabin opened.

Michelle gulped and stared up into the face of Ms. Greene—the camp director!

"What are you girls doing?" Ms. Greene asked.

"Uh—nothing!" Megan said quickly.

Out of the corner of her eye, Michelle saw Sunny scurry into Ms. Greene's cabin!

Beside her, Megan gasped. She had seen him go in, too.

Ms. Greene let the door to her cabin swing shut behind her. She glanced at her watch. "You girls should be heading down to the lake now," she said. "It's time for the swimming test."

"Oh, right," Megan said. "That's where we were going."

Ms. Greene raised an eyebrow. "Are you planning to swim in your shorts?"

"Oh—of course not," Michelle said. "Come on, Megan. We'd better hurry and change."

"I'll walk with you," Ms. Greene said. "I don't want you girls to be late."

Michelle groaned as she and Megan dashed into their cabin to change into their suits.

"Sunny is in Ms. Greene's cabin!" Megan whispered. "What are we going to do now?"

"We'll have to sneak in there and get Sunny back," Michelle decided. "Before Ms. Greene finds him!"

Chapter
5

♥   Michelle stood on the dock, staring into the water. Her mind was filled with images of Sunny's trusting little face and twitchy nose. She just had to get him back—no matter what.

"Michelle! Hey, Michelle!" Megan called out. "Are you afraid to jump?"

"What?" Michelle shook her head. She stared at her new friend treading water in the lake below.

Lauren walked up beside Michelle and laid a reassuring hand on her shoulder. "Are you scared of the water?" she asked softly. "It's okay. I'll take you over to the shallow side of the lake."

"Oh, no!" Michelle blushed. "I love to swim! I—I was just thinking about something." She turned back to the water. "Look out below!" she shouted at Megan. Then she jumped in.

Both Michelle and Megan passed the swim test with flying colors. They got red swim caps, which meant they were in the highest-level swimming group.

When the swim test was over, Lauren led her whole group back to their cabin. After quick showers and a change, it was time for dinner.

"There's no time to look for Sunny now," Megan whispered to Michelle.

"Cross your fingers and hope for the best," Michelle answered. "Maybe we'll have a chance after dinner."

"Come on, girls, let's go eat. The first girl who can guess what's on her plate wins a prize," Lauren joked.

The food at dinner was actually pretty good— burgers, fries, and a salad. But when Michelle looked at her plate, she got a lump in her throat.

Sunny loves lettuce, she thought.

"Are you going to eat your fries?" Taylor asked.

Michelle shook her head.

"Can I have them?"

"Sure." Michelle shoved her plate across the table.

After dinner there was a movie. Michelle was going to sneak out to go find Sunny. But Ms.

Greene sat in a chair by the door. There was no other way out.

On the way back to their cabin, Michelle and her friends passed the director's cabin. Michelle stood on tiptoes and tried to look in the window as they walked past. But the inside of the cabin was dark. She couldn't see anything. Besides, if Sunny was still in there, he was way down on the floor.

"Hey, everybody!" Brianna shouted. "Look at Michelle!"

Michelle whirled around.

"She's walking like a ballerina!" Brianna stood on tiptoe like Michelle and walked along the path. "Let's do funny walks all the way back to the cabin!"

"Cool!" Lateesha said, copying Brianna.

Lauren and the rest of the girls took turns coming up with funny walks. Lateesha walked backward. Taylor made everyone walk with both hands clasped behind one knee.

"Do you think Sunny is still in Ms. Greene's cabin?" Megan whispered in Michelle's ear as they hobbled down the path.

"I couldn't see him, but I hope so," Michelle whispered.

"What do we do now?" Megan whispered again.

"We'll have to sneak into Ms. Greene's cabin after lights out," Michelle told her friend.

Megan's eyes grew wide. "Sneak in? Are you crazy?"

"It's our only chance," Michelle answered.

Michelle thought her cabin mates would never get to sleep that night. First Krysta started a pillow fight. Then Lateesha wanted to tell ghost stories.

Finally Lauren made everyone go to bed. "Hit the sack, guys," she said. "Ms. Greene is really strict about lights out."

Michelle crawled into bed, yawning loudly. "I'm *so* sleepy!" she said. She hoped she could get everybody else yawning, too.

It took awhile, but at last the cabin was quiet. Michelle reached up to Megan's bunk and poked her in the leg.

Quiet as a mouse, Megan slipped down from her bunk. Her feet didn't even make a sound as she touched the floor.

Together they tiptoed to the screen door. Michelle took the handle. Inch by inch she eased open the door. She was nearly through when—

Squeak!

Michelle froze and listened. Someone on a top bunk turned over. Luckily, the noise didn't wake anybody up.

Michelle peeked at Lauren in her bottom bunk by the door. Had *she* heard the noise?

25

Nope. The counselor didn't move.

Bravely Michelle and Megan stepped out into the dark night. Outside, the three-quarter moon lit their way to Ms. Greene's cabin.

There was no light on inside the cabin, Michelle noticed. That was a good sign. She held out a hand for Megan to stop.

"What are we waiting for?" Megan whispered.

"We have to make sure Ms. Greene is asleep," Michelle told her. She crept up next to the cabin window and listened.

"Zzzzzzz . . ."

Michelle smiled. Ms. Greene was snoring like a bear!

Megan covered her mouth to smother a giggle.

"You stand watch," Michelle whispered. "I'm going in!"

Megan faced the path while Michelle sneaked to the door and slid inside the cabin.

The hair on the back of Michelle's neck prickled as she looked around. This was going to be harder than she expected. It was so dark that she could hardly see! And Ms. Greene could wake up any minute. What would she say? How could she explain?

Michelle glanced around the room. Moonlight shone in through the screened windows like soft dim spotlights. Where would a tiny guinea pig hide? she wondered.

Suddenly Michelle heard the faintest sound—like tiny teeth chewing on something crunchy. She peeked under the camp director's desk. There, behind the trash can, Sunny was munching on some peanut shells that had fallen on the floor.

Michelle nearly whooped with relief. She clamped her mouth shut and quietly scooped Sunny into her hands. Then slowly she tiptoed back to the door.

Holding Sunny to her chest with one hand, she reached for the door handle with the other and pulled open the screen.

A loud snort came from Ms. Greene's bed. Michelle froze and waited. Oh, no! she thought. Is Ms. Greene waking up?

No, the camp director had just shifted in her bed. Michelle hurried out the door.

"Michelle!" Megan said. "You did it! I was so scared!"

Michelle blew out a breath. "I can't believe I—"

A light, bobbing down the path, interrupted Michelle's thought.

Megan grabbed Michelle's arm. "What is that?" she asked.

Michelle peered through the night. "Uh-oh, Megan. It's someone with a flashlight!"

"Lauren!" Megan whispered.

"She must have noticed that we were gone,"

Michelle said. "I bet she's looking for us. Come on!" Michelle grabbed Megan's arm and ran farther away from the cabins. Seconds later they came to the dining hall.

Michelle spotted a gray door at the side of the building. "Quick!" she whispered. "In here!"

The two girls ducked inside.

"Where are we?" Megan whispered.

In the moonlight Michelle could make out a huge refrigerator and stove. "We're in the kitchen," she reported.

She glanced around and noticed a door standing open in the room. She jogged over to it—it was the supply closet.

Michelle quickly scanned the shelves. They were filled with all kinds of pots and pans and other cooking supplies.

She grabbed a tall silver pot—the kind her dad used to cook spaghetti. Sunny would never be able to climb up the steep slick sides and escape from *this*. She handed the pot to Megan, then tucked Sunny inside.

Michelle opened the refrigerator and looked around. There! Just what I need! she thought. Lettuce! She pulled off several leaves and put them into the pot with Sunny.

"You'd better leave the lid open a little—so he can get some air," Megan warned.

"Good idea." Michelle carefully placed the lid halfway on, then she stuck the pot back in the supply closet. Sunny would be safe in there until the next morning.

"Good night, Sunny!" Michelle whispered. She promised herself that the next day she would get up before everyone else in camp to move Sunny back to her cabin.

She closed the supply closet doors and tiptoed out of the dining hall with Megan.

Not far down the path they could see that Lauren was still searching for them. Her flashlight bobbed as she strode up the path—right toward Megan and Michelle.

"We're caught!" Michelle said.

"Not yet," Megan whispered. "Play along."

Lauren jogged up to them, a worried look on her face. "Michelle! Megan!" she said. "What are you doing out here in the middle of the night?"

Michelle glanced sideways at Megan. Her eyes were half closed. She held her hands out in front of her. She stumbled forward sleepily, as if she had no idea where she was.

"Oh! Megan's . . . uh . . . sleepwalking!" Michelle said, finally catching on. "I heard her leave the cabin. So I came out after her." She slipped an arm around Megan's shoulders. "My sister Stephanie does this all the time. My dad

29

says don't wake her up. Just take her back to bed."

Lauren looked at the two girls uncertainly. Then she nodded and led them back to their cabin. "I'm just glad we didn't wake up Ms. Greene," she whispered as she opened the cabin door.

"Me, too!" Michelle said. *Really* glad!"

Michelle helped Megan climb into her top bunk, and then she slipped into her own bed.

Sunny is safe, Michelle thought. At least for now. And the sooner I go to sleep, the sooner I can get up and put him back in my cabin where he belongs!

"Michelle! Michelle—wake up!"

Michelle pulled her head up from the pillow. It was morning already. "What time is it?" she asked

"Late," Megan whispered. "Everybody has already left for breakfast!"

"Breakfast. Oh, no! I overslept!" Michelle jumped out of bed and threw on some shorts and a T-shirt. "Come on!" she told Megan. "We've got to find out if Sunny's okay!"

They rushed to the dining hall and burst into the kitchen through the side door.

Michelle looked up—and gasped in horror!

Steam rose from a boiling pot—

The same pot she had hidden Sunny in!

Oh, no!

Sunny was cooked!

Chapter 6

♥   "No!" Michelle yelled. She rushed to the stove to look in the pot.

"Girls!" the cook exclaimed. "Be careful! You could get hurt!"

"But—I need to see what's in that pot!" Michelle said.

The cook stared at Michelle for a second. "It's just boiling water, honey. I'm making some more oatmeal." She lifted the lid, and Michelle peered in the pot.

Whew! It was just boiling water in there. Michelle nearly fainted with relief. Sunny wasn't there.

"Of course he's not there," Megan said as they headed into the dining hall. "The cook would have seen him when she ran water into the pot. Sunny must have escaped sometime during the night."

Michelle groaned. "That means he could have run off anywhere. We're right back where we started!"

Michelle and Megan got their breakfast, but Michelle wasn't hungry. She poked at her oatmeal. Poor Sunny! she thought. He might be scared. He might be hungry! How can I eat when it's all my fault?

"Michelle, are you all right?"

Michelle looked up into the eyes of Lauren, her counselor. "I'm fine," she said quickly.

"Are you sure?" Lauren said. "I noticed you've haven't been eating very much." She leaned closer and whispered, "Are you feeling a little home-sick?"

Michelle gazed up into Lauren's face. Her eyes looked kind and concerned. Could she trust her? Could she tell Lauren her secret about Sunny? It would feel so good to tell *somebody* what was going on.

Then she remembered about Megan's cousin— the one who was sent home because of her bunny. "No, I'm fine," Michelle said.

"Well, I'm here if you feel like talking," Lauren said. "Okay?"

Michelle nodded and tried to smile.

But inside she felt like crying. Where could Sunny be now?

The morning schedule was busy. There was no time to slip away and search for Sunny. In arts and crafts Michelle was so worried, she could hardly pay attention to her project.

Everyone was sitting in the big meeting room making twig picture frames. Michelle glued and glued without really looking at what she was doing.

"Very interesting," Lauren said when she came by to look at Michelle's work. "A picture frame with eight sides."

Oops, Michelle thought. I didn't mean to do that! I'd better pay closer attention, or Lauren might guess that something's up!

"Pretty cool, Michelle!" Megan said. "I'm going to make a frame just like yours." She pulled her twigs apart and started over.

"Hey, me, too," Taylor said. Soon a bunch of Michelle's cabin mates were making odd-shaped frames.

Michelle glanced down. Wouldn't a picture of Sunny look nice in my frame? she thought. A tear slipped from her eye, and she wiped it away. A picture might be the only way I ever get to see Sunny again!

Michelle reached for a paper towel to wipe her

nose, and knocked a plastic glue bottle onto the floor. "Sorry, guys," she mumbled.

She leaned over to pick up the bottle. Then froze.

That's strange, she thought. There were little spots of paint across the floor. Spots that looked almost like . . . tiny little footprints!

Tiny little guinea pig feet might make footprints like that! Michelle thought. A tiny little guinea pig like Sunny!

Michelle jumped up from her seat and followed the footprints across the floor. They led right into a closet.

Michelle dashed over. The door was open just a crack. Quickly she flung open the door.

A furry little guinea pig stared up at her from the floor.

"Sunny!" she whispered.

She dropped to her knees and scooped the little guinea pig into her arms. "You poor thing! I'm so sorry. Are you all right? Are you starving?" She peered into his big black eyes. He seemed perfectly fine.

Just then Michelle felt someone walk up behind her.

Uh-oh, Michelle thought.

"Michelle, what are you doing with that guinea pig?" she heard Lauren say.

Michelle gulped.

Busted!

Chapter

7

♥   "Michelle, I asked you a question," Lauren continued. "What are you doing with that guinea pig? Is it yours?"

Quick! Michelle told herself. Make up an excuse! Tell her you just found Sunny. Tell her you don't know who he belongs to! Tell her he's actually a wild chipmunk!

Michelle opened her mouth to tell some kind of fib. Anything to keep from getting into trouble. Anything to keep from getting sent home!

Instead, she let out a long slow breath. She was tired. Tired of not telling the truth. Tired of hiding!

And suddenly she was blurting out everything.

"Yes," she said. "It's my guinea pig. I didn't

mean to bring him. See, my friend Lee was going to look after him. Only he couldn't at the last minute, so he brought Sunny to me at the bus. Then you blew the whistle and I had to get *on* the bus, and, I didn't know what else to do so—so I brought him with me."

She paused. "I guess you think I'm terrible now. I guess you're going to tell Ms. Greene I have a pet at camp, and then she'll send me home—right?"

To Michelle's surprise, Lauren smiled. It was one of the biggest, widest smiles Michelle had ever seen. "Oh, I don't know if we have to tell Ms. Greene anything."

"Huh? Why not?" Michelle asked.

Then Lauren reached into her shirt pocket and pulled something out.

Michelle gasped. It was a tiny squirming lizard!

"Meet Herman," Lauren said, laughing. "He's my pet, and I don't think he'd want you or Sunny to get in trouble."

"Cool!" Michelle said. "Sunny, it looks like we are going to have a great time at camp for the rest of the week!

Michelle's
Cool Camp Guide
and
Fun Book

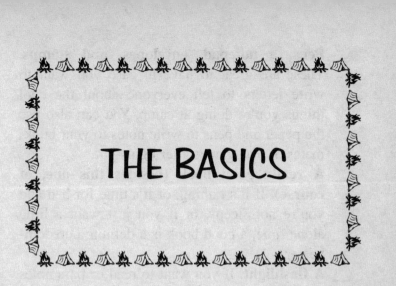

THE BASICS

What to Bring

Wow! You're actually going to camp! You'll have a great time. Before you throw on your backpack and step into the great outdoors, you have to *pack!* Your camp will probably send a list of things that you need to bring with you. But here are some other handy items that you might want to carry along:

Your pillow. There's nothing like snuggling up with your own sweet pillow to keep homesickness away. If you don't want to lug your pillow, a favorite stuffed animal can work, too.

📖 **Pens, a notepad, envelopes, and stamps.** These are great to have in case you want to write letters to tell everyone about the cool things you're doing at camp. You can also use the paper and pens to write notes to your bunkmates or play games after lights-out.

📖 **A really good book (besides this one, of course).** If it's raining, or it's time for bed and you're not sleepy, or if you just want a little alone time, a good book is a definite boredom-beater.

📖 **A flashlight.** If you want to read or pass notes after lights-out, it helps to be able to see. Don't forget the batteries!

📖 **Lip balm.** Chapped lips are no fun—so be prepared.

📖 **A disposable camera.** This is great because you can take it everywhere and snap pictures of all your camp buddies. And if you lose your camera, you've only lost your pictures, not a ton of money!

Wait! Before you zip up that suitcase, here's a list of things you'll need if you want to do some of the activities in this book:

☆ Ten or so sheets of 81/2-by-11-inch plain white paper

☆ A white pillowcase or T-shirt
☆ Permanent fabric pens. Just one color is fine, but if you can get a bunch of colors, that's even better.
☆ Balloons—the round kind are best
☆ Embroidery thread—four different colors
☆ Tape
☆ A ruler

What Not to Bring

Here are just a few things you'll be better off leaving at home:

🐢 **Anything expensive or valuable.** Besides jewelry and money, this includes anything that you would be really sad if you lost.

🐢 **A bad attitude.** You might be a little scared if you've never been to camp before. If you arrive at camp expecting trouble, you'll probably find it. But don't worry! Act like your normal friendly self, and camp will be a breeze.

🐢 **Pets—like guinea pigs!**

How to Make Friends

Whew! Now you're packed and your parents have dropped you off at camp. You're probably thinking that this is going to the best summer EVER! But don't freak if you're just a teensy bit worried about meeting all of those new people. Will you make friends? Of course you will! Remember, all of those other campers want to make friends, too. Here are some hints on how to get started:

1. Smile and say, "Hi." A happy face makes other people feel happy, too. If someone smiles and says hi to you, isn't it pretty hard not to say hi back?

2. So you've introduced yourself. Can't think of anything else to say? The best trick is to ask questions. "Where are you from?" "What grade are you in?" "Is this your first time at camp?" "Where did you get that neat T-shirt?" "What's your favorite sport?" Before you know it, you'll find out something you both have in common.

3. Now what? Go do something together! Go swimming. Save each other a seat in the dining hall. Play hangman or tic-tac-toe during rest time. By the time you leave camp, that stranger will be a friend you'll hate to say goodbye to!

Help! I'm Homesick!

Okay, you're on your way to making friends. But what if you get homesick? If you start to really miss your mom, your dad, your pet, your bed—whatever? Don't get bummed out. Here are a few ideas to get you through it:

1. Make a list of all the things you like about camp. Write down all your favorites, such as: What activities do you love? Where's the coolest spot to hang out? Who's the nicest counselor? You get the idea. It will help you see that, hey, camp is pretty awesome!
2. If your camp allows it, call or e-mail home. Sometimes just hearing your mom or dad's voice can make you feel like everything's okay. Even writing a letter can make you feel better.
3. Stay busy. Go swimming, work on a cool craft, take a walk, or play a game with campmates. You may have so much to do that you'll totally forget to be homesick!

BUNKMATES

Feeling shy with your new friends? That's just because you don't know them yet. Here are some fun ways to get to know your bunkmates—fast!

❀ Play Two Truths and a Lie. Have everyone sit together in a circle. Beginning with yourself, each camper tells two things that are true about herself and one thing that's not true. The other bunkmates have to guess which ones are true and which one isn't. You can make the untrue things little fibs—like you have a dog instead of a cat. Or you can tell your bunkmates a whopper—like your family is from Venus. You choose!

❀ If your cabin doesn't already have a name, come up with one. Make it cool! Make it fun and flashy! Try to come up with something that describes all of your bunkmates, like "Supergrrrlz" or "Sweet-n-Sassy." Then make a poster with the name on it and decorate it. (You can do this even if your cabin already has a name.) Have all of your bunkmates autograph it and hang it up to tell everyone exactly who you are!

❀ You and your new bunk buddies probably have a lot in common. You just don't know it yet. Maybe you have the same number of sisters and brothers. Or maybe you like the same kind of music or books. Break out your pens and notepad (aren't you glad you packed them?) and have everyone write down her favorite things. **Hint:** Some good favorites to write down are Food, Color, TV Show, Book, Subject at School, Sport, After-School Activity, Movie, Actor, Actress, Music Group, and Animal.

❀ Don't put your names on the papers. When everyone has finished, put the papers in a stack, facedown. Take one off the top and read the list aloud. Then see if you can guess who the list belongs to!

45

STUFF TO DO

So you've made friends, now what? Although there are tons of things to do at camp, you're bound to have some down time. If you find yourself with nothing to do, try some of these fun things with your new buddies!

Make a Fortune Catcher

What does the future hold? Follow the instructions below to turn a simple piece of paper into a Fortune Catcher!

What you need:

✄ A sheet of plain white 8½-by-11-inch paper

✄ A pen or pencil
✄ Scissors
✄ A ruler

What you do:

1. Cut your paper into a square that measures 8½ inches by 8½ inches.
2. Fold your paper into quarters. You can do this by folding it in half once lengthwise. Then, fold it in half once width-wise. (Your paper should now look like a smaller square.) Open up your paper. You should see a cross in the paper where you made your folds.
3. Next, take the upper right-hand corner of the paper and fold it in so that it touches the center, where the two lines of the cross meet. Do this to the other three corners.

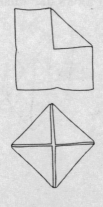

4. Flip over your folded paper. Now, take the upper right-hand corner, and fold it into the center. Do this to the other three corners.

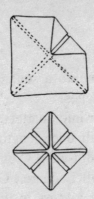

5. Then, take the bottom edge of the paper and fold it so that it touches the top edge. Slip the thumbs and index fingers of both hands underneath the flaps on the bottom of your folded paper and pinch toward the center. You should now have something that looks like this.

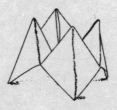

6. Whew! Your Fortune Catcher is almost finished. Now you need to fill it with fortunes. Lay your Fortune Catcher flat on a table so that the four square flaps are facing up. Write the name of a color on each square such as red, blue, green, and yellow.

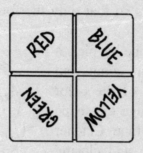

7. Flip over your Fortune Catcher so that the four triangular flaps are facing up. They should be divided into eight sections by a folded line. Write a number from one to eight on each section.
8. Then, open up the triangular flaps and write silly fortunes on the underside of each numbered section.

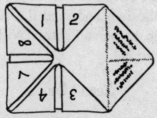

You can write things like: You will be super rich

49

when you grow up. *Or:* You will marry the first boy you kiss. Use your imagination. Have fun!

How to play:

1. Fold the Fortune Catcher back up and slip it over your fingers so that only the four colored areas are shown.

2. Ask someone to pick a color, then count out each letter of the color name. Change the shape of the Fortune Catcher by opening and closing it in opposite directions.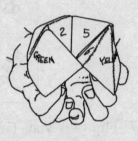

3. Then ask the person to pick a number shown in the center of the Fortune Catcher, and count it out as you change the shape of the Fortune Catcher again.

4. Finally ask the person to pick another number shown in the open Fortune Catcher.

5. Open up the flap and read the fortune beneath the number the person chose. Will it come true? You never know!

Secret Code

Use this password code to write super-secret notes for your bunkmates!

What you need:

✏ A piece of paper
✏ A pen

What you do:

To make this code, write down the entire alphabet in a single row on a piece of paper. Pick a secret password that doesn't repeat any letters—like the word "FRIENDS" or "PRIVATE"—and write it down underneath the first row of letters. Then write down the rest of the alphabet after your secret word, leaving out the letters in the secret word. (Remember—you've already used them!) Be careful to put one letter beneath each letter in the first row.

ROW 1: A B C D E F G H I J K L M N O P Q R S T U V W X Y Z
ROW 2: F R I E N D S A B C G H J K L M O P Q T U V W X Y Z

Use the letters in the second row to write your note. For example, if you wanted to spell the word *dog,* you would write E instead of D, L instead of O, and S instead of G. The sentence "Meet me before dinner" would look like this in your secret code: JNNT JN RNDLPN EBKKNP.

Puzzle Power

Camp just wouldn't be the same without scary stories told in the dark, right? Here's a crazy fill-in story that you can do with your bunkmates. Just grab a few friends and ask them to answer the questions in the list below without showing them the story. Fill in the numbered blanks in the story with the answers your friends came up with. Then read the story aloud. You might want to leave the lights on because this story might make you scream . . . with laughter!

1. A word to describe a monster
2. The name of your camp
3. A size
4. A number
5. A word to describe something you don't like
6. A girl's name
7. A height
8. A color
9. Another color
10. A fun camp activity
11. A word to describe something you like

12. A group of objects (like dogs, students, or rocks)
13. An activity you dislike
14. A word to describe something scary
15. Another group of things
16. A word to describe the way something smells
17. Your answer from question #15
18. A thing
19. Something a ghost does
20. Something you yell out

The Absolutely True Story of the _____
(#1)

Monster of Camp _____ !
(#2)

I swear this _____ story is absolutely true!
(#3)

Once, about _____ years ago, there was a
(#4)

_____ young camper named _____.
(#5)   (#6)

She was _____ with _____ hair
(#7)   (#8)

and _____ eyes. She never wanted to
(#9)

_____ or join in any of the _____
(#10)   (#11)

games with the other _____. Instead she spent
(#12)

all her time _____ and playing _____
(#13)   (#14)

tricks on the rest of the _____. One day
(#15)

she wandered into the _____ woods and
(#16)

disappeared. All the _____ got together
                            (#17)

to look for her, but all they ever found was her

_____. It's said that she still _____
       (#18)   (#19)

the woods to this day, sneaking up behind unlucky

campers, and shouting "_____!"
                              (#20)

A Camp-y Word Search

Save this word search to cheer you up on a cloudy afternoon. See if you can find all of the camp-y words in the puzzle below. Words go up, down, forward, backward, and diagonally.

S	O	N	G	S	M	R	I	G	H	T
W	L	A	K	E	O	M	E	C	O	M
I	B	E	T	H	S	I	C	L	Y	I
M	F	A	E	T	Q	N	F	R	E	D
M	L	N	C	P	U	D	U	G	G	E
I	G	I	F	R	I	E	N	D	S	U
N	N	B	A	B	T	N	E	I	S	C
G	I	A	S	L	O	V	G	U	T	K
B	K	C	A	P	K	C	A	B	R	R
O	I	J	O	E	V	S	I	O	A	O
N	H	C	R	A	F	T	S	I	V	G

ARTS   HIKING
BACKPACK   LAKE
CABIN   MOSQUITO
CRAFTS   SLEEPING BAG
FRIENDS   SONGS
FUN   SWIMMING

ANSWER ON PAGE 67

55

Pass and Splash!

If it's just too darn hot, play a "cool" game of Pass and Splash.

What you need:

❋ Balloons
❋ Water
❋ A bathing suit!

What you do:

Fill up a bunch of balloons with water. Tie a knot at the opening of the balloon. Pass one out to each player.

How to play:

Have everyone stand in a circle and pass her balloon to the right as fast as she can. A player can have only one balloon in her hand at a time, so keep passing!

If a player drops her balloon and it breaks, she's out. If it doesn't break, she has to pick it up and hurry back into the game. The last one dry is a rotten egg!

FRIENDS FOREVER

The last day of camp is coming near. You've made all these great new friends, and soon you'll have to say goodbye. Here are some fun ways to remember camp forever and keep in touch with all of your new friends.

Friendship Bracelets

These bracelets are so cool. And they're not hard to make at all! They're basically just a fancy braid. A little advice: These are way easier to make if you use four different colors. In these instructions, we'll use red, blue, yellow, and green threads.

What you need:

♥ Four two-foot strands of embroidery thread
(Note: Embroidery thread is actually made up
of about six or eight separate strings, woven
together. Don't pull the strings apart or you'll
end up with a mess!)

♥ Tape

What you do:

1. Tie the four strands of
thread together in a knot
about two inches from the
top. Tape the knotted end
securely to the edge of a
table so you can keep the
threads tight. The threads
should go left to right in
this order: red, blue, yellow, and green.

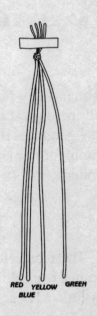

RED   YELLOW   GREEN
BLUE

2. Make your first knot by bringing the red thread over the blue thread so that the two threads form a number four (see illustration). Then pass the red thread underneath the green thread and pull it tight.

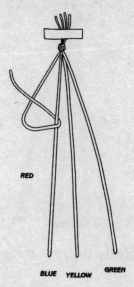

RED

BLUE YELLOW GREEN

Do this twice to make a double knot. Take the red string again and do the same thing with the yellow string. Then do it again with the green string. The first row is done!

3. Start the second row by taking the blue string (it should be on the far left now) and making a double knot around the yellow string, then the green

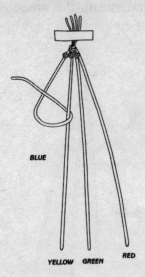

string, and finally the red string. That's the second row!
4. Keep making rows by starting with the string on the far left and working your way to the right. When your bracelet is about five or six inches long (or long enough to fit around your wrist comfortably), tie a knot in the bottom end so the strings don't unravel.
5. The last step? Give it to your friend!

Memory Pillow

Have your camp buddies help you make a memory pillow so you can dream about camp all year long! (Or if you'd rather *wear* your memories, make a memory T-shirt.)

What you need:

◇ A plain white pillowcase (or T-shirt)
◇ A permanent fabric marker
◇ A piece of cardboard

What you do:

Spread out your pillowcase and put the cardboard inside to keep the ink from bleeding through. Then have all your friends write something on the pillowcase using the fabric markers. They can write their names, nicknames, poems, short notes, or even their addresses and phone numbers. When the ink is totally dry, you can take out the cardboard, slip your pillowcase onto your pillow, and get ready for dreamcamp!

Michelle's Picture Frame

Here's another great way to take summer camp home with you. Make a cool twig picture frame and remember the fun you had at camp all year long!

What you need:

❁ A ruler
❁ Four twigs—two about three inches long and two about five inches long.
❁ Glue

What you do:

While you're out in the woods, keep your eyes peeled for interesting twigs. Look for ones on the ground—don't break them off living trees or bushes. When you've collected at least four, you're ready to make your frame!

To do this, place the two three-inch twigs side by side on a table about five inches apart from each other. Then place the two five-inch twigs across the three-inch twigs so that they form a rectangle. Use your ruler to make sure the hole measures three inches high and five inches wide. Then apply glue to each corner and wait for it to dry.

When you get home, pick out a favorite picture of

you and your bunkmates. Put a thin strip of glue along all four edges on the front of the picture and press it into the frame. Wait for the glue to dry, then prop up your newly framed photo to remind yourself of all the fun you had!

Address Pages

Hold on! This isn't the end! Keep in touch with all your new friends. Write their names, addresses, phone numbers, and e-mail addresses in the spaces below. Drop them a note and let them know how you're doing!

Friend's name: _____

Home address: _____

_____

Phone number: _____

E-mail address: _____

Friend's name: _____

Home address: _____

_____

Phone number: _____

E-mail address: _____

Friend's name: _____

Home address: _____

_____

Phone number: _____

E-mail address: _____

Friend's name: _____

Home address: _____

_____

Phone number: _____

E-mail address: _____

Friend's name: _____

Home address: _____

_____

Phone number: _____

E-mail address: _____

Friend's name: _____

Home address: _____

_____

Phone number: _____

E-mail address: _____

Friend's name: _____

Home address: _____

_____

Phone number: _____

E-mail address: _____

S	O	N	G	S	M	R	I	G	H	T
W	L	A	K	E	O	M	E	C	O	M
I	B	E	T	H	S	I	C	L	Y	I
M	F	A	E	T	Q	N	F	R	E	D
M	L	N	C	P	U	D	U	G	G	E
I	G	I	F	R	I	E	N	D	S	U
N	N	B	A	B	T	N	E	I	S	C
G	I	A	S	L	O	V	G	U	T	K
B	K	C	A	P	K	C	A	B	R	R
O	I	J	O	E	V	S	I	O	A	O
N	H	C	R	A	F	T	S	I	V	G

FULL HOUSE™
Michelle

A MINSTREL® BOOK
Published by Pocket Books

1033-36

Don't miss out on any of
Stephanie and Michelle's
exciting adventures!

FULL HOUSE™
Sisters

*When sisters get together...
expect the unexpected!*

A MINSTREL® BOOK
Published by Pocket Books

It doesn't matter if you live around the corner...
or around the world...
If you are a fan of Mary-Kate and Ashley Olsen,
you should be a member of

MARY-KATE + ASHLEY'S FUN CLUB™

Here's what you get:
Our Funzine™
An autographed color photo
Two black & white individual photos
A full size color poster
An official **Fun Club**™ membership card
A **Fun Club**™ school folder
Two special **Fun Club**™ surprises
A holiday card
Fun Club™ collectibles catalog
Plus a **Fun Club**™ box to keep everything in

To join Mary-Kate + Ashley's Fun Club™, fill out the form
below and send it along with

U.S. Residents – $17.00
Canadian Residents – $22 U.S. Funds
International Residents – $27 U.S. Funds

MARY-KATE + ASHLEY'S FUN CLUB™
859 HOLLYWOOD WAY, SUITE 275
BURBANK, CA 91505

NAME:_____

ADDRESS:_____

_CITY:_____ STATE:_____ ZIP:_____

PHONE:(____) _____ BIRTHDATE:_____